MW00933796

So That's What God Is Like!

Story by **LeAnne Hardy**

Illustrated by **Janet Wilson**

So That's What God Is Like

Text © 2004 by LeAnne Hardy
Illustrations © 2004 by Janet Wilson

Published by Kregel Kidzone, an imprint of Kregel Publications, P.O. Box 2607, Grand Rapids, MI 49501.

All rights reserved. No part of this book may be reproduced, stored in a retrieval system, or transmitted in any form or by any means—electronic, mechanical, photocopy, recording, or otherwise—without written permission of the publisher, except for brief quotations in printed reviews.

Scripture quotations are from the *Holy Bible, New International Version*®. © 1973, 1978, 1984 by International Bible Society. Used by permission of Zondervan Publishing House. All rights reserved.

The borders featured in this book are representative of the beadwork of the Zulu people of South Africa.

Art Direction / Interior Design: John M. Lucas

ISBN 0-8254-2782-7

Printed in China

1 2 3 4 5 / 08 07 06 05 04

For Steven,
who believed in this story.
—L. H.

For Jenny.
Also, many thanks and
appreciation to the Badoe family.
—J. W.

Temba was the smallest in his family
except for baby Hannah.

When Temba took care of the goats with his big brother Sipo, his legs were too short to leap from rock to rock. He had to climb down and clamber up the next rock.

When Mama carried a heavy tin of water on her head to the tiny corn plants in the garden, Temba could only carry a little can. Most of the water spilled on Temba.

Temba loved to go to church with Granny. Granny had the biggest voice in the choir.

He liked to hear the stories his Sunday school teacher told from the big Bible she carried.

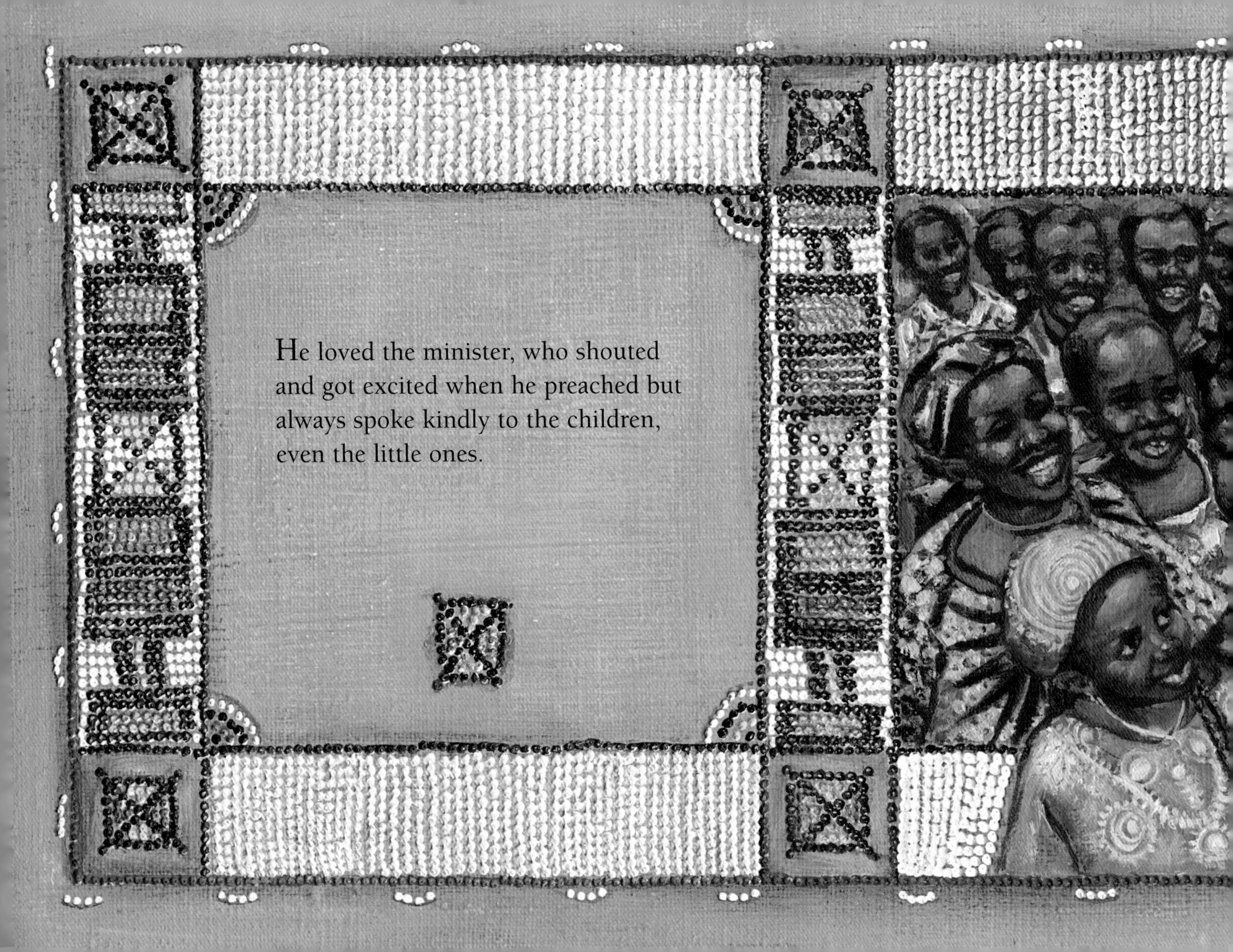

He loved the minister, who shouted and got excited when he preached but always spoke kindly to the children, even the little ones.

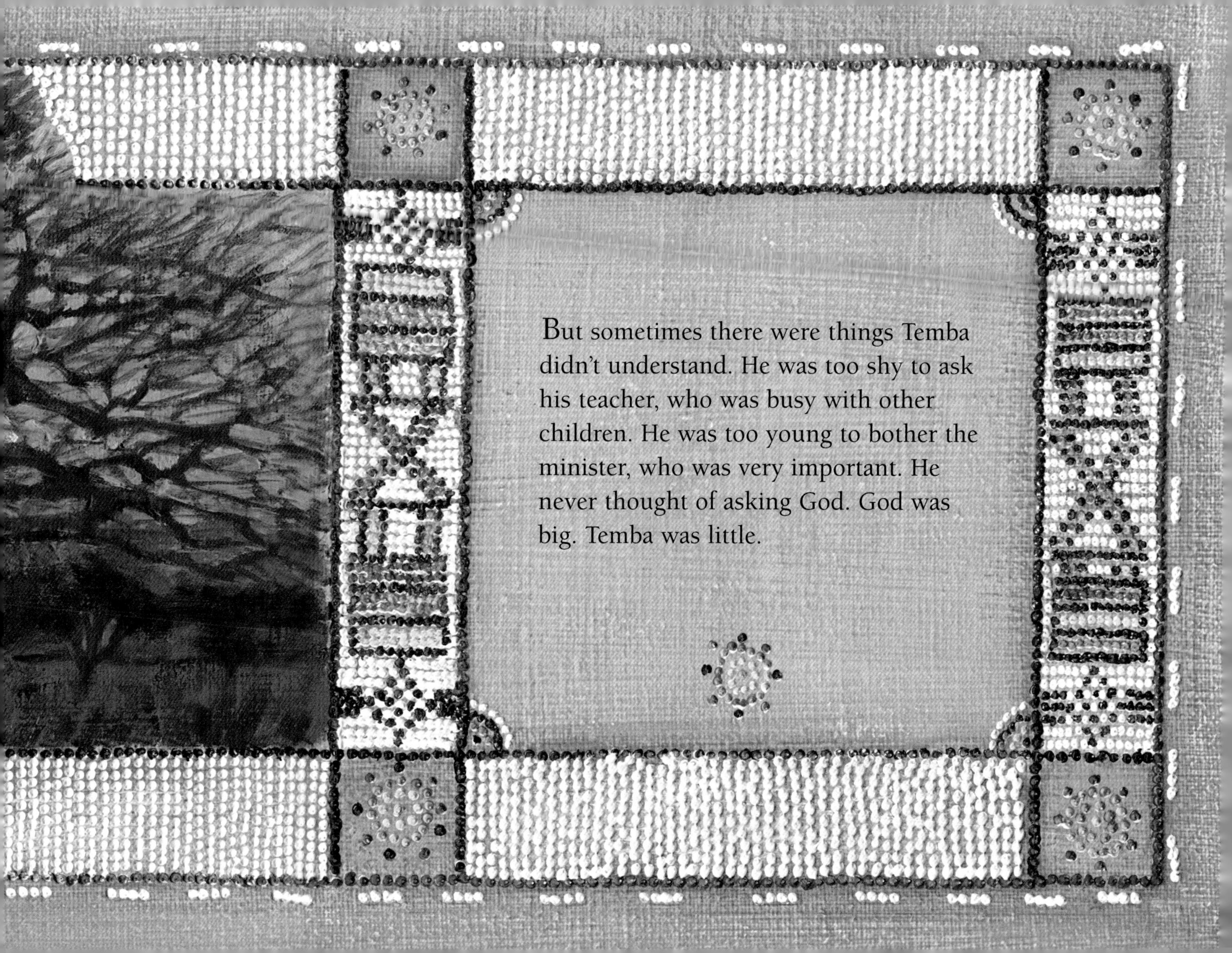

But sometimes there were things Temba didn't understand. He was too shy to ask his teacher, who was busy with other children. He was too young to bother the minister, who was very important. He never thought of asking God. God was big. Temba was little.

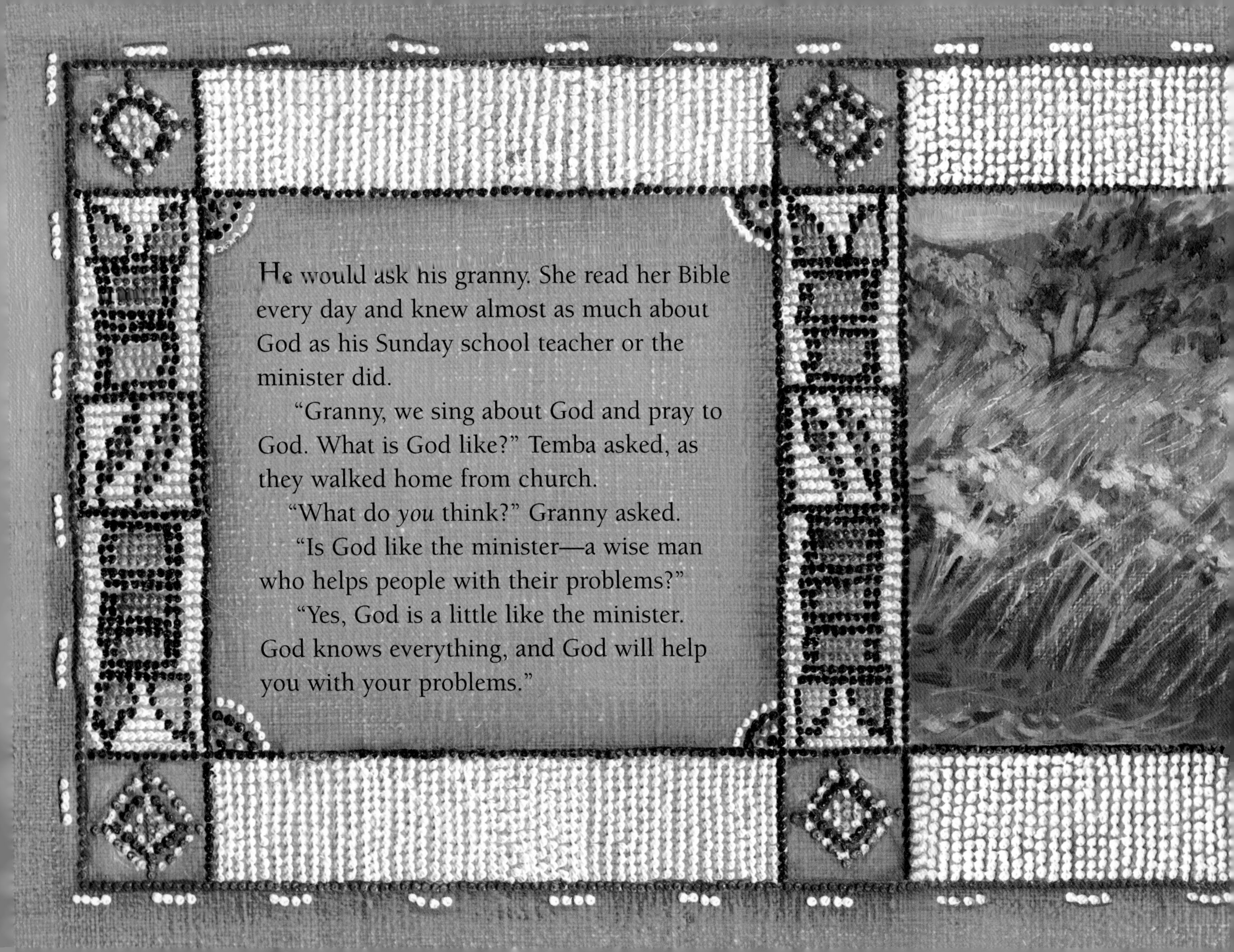

He would ask his granny. She read her Bible every day and knew almost as much about God as his Sunday school teacher or the minister did.

"Granny, we sing about God and pray to God. What is God like?" Temba asked, as they walked home from church.

"What do *you* think?" Granny asked.

"Is God like the minister—a wise man who helps people with their problems?"

"Yes, God is a little like the minister. God knows everything, and God will help you with your problems."

Cast all your anxiety on him
because he cares for you.
—1 Peter 5:7

"The wind blows wherever it pleases.
You hear its sound, but you cannot tell
where it comes from or where it is going.
So it is with everyone born of the Spirit."
—John 3:8

"But God is not exactly like the minister," Granny explained, "because God is not a man."

Temba cocked his head and thought hard.

"God is a spirit," Granny said.

A hot wind blew off the plain. The leaves rustled in the trees around them, and Granny had to hold onto her hat. "A spirit is like the wind. You can't see it, but you know that it's there."

Temba chased a ball of fluff from the silk cotton tree as it blew down the road. "So that's what God is like," he said.

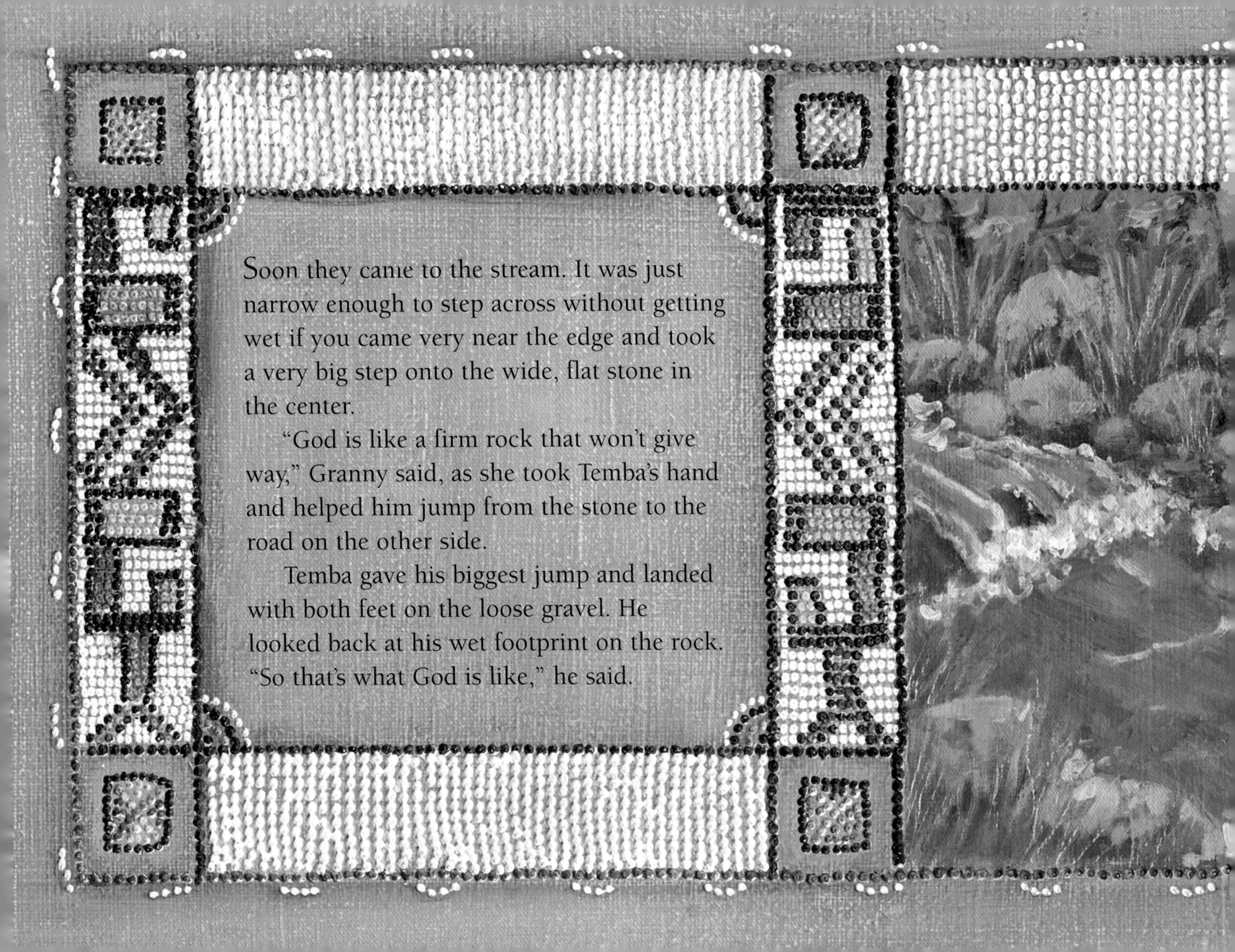

Soon they came to the stream. It was just narrow enough to step across without getting wet if you came very near the edge and took a very big step onto the wide, flat stone in the center.

"God is like a firm rock that won't give way," Granny said, as she took Temba's hand and helped him jump from the stone to the road on the other side.

Temba gave his biggest jump and landed with both feet on the loose gravel. He looked back at his wet footprint on the rock. "So that's what God is like," he said.

He set my feet on a rock and gave me a firm place to stand.
—Psalm 40:2

"How often I have longed to gather your children together, as a hen gathers her chicks under her wings."
—Matthew 23:37

Temba and Granny came near their own farm. There was Mama's speckled hen, teaching her chicks to scratch outside the thornbush fence. The mother hen clucked furiously, calling her little ones into the shelter of the thorns.

A stray dog trotted over and sniffed at the hen in the thorns. He gave a sharp yelp of pain and backed away, rubbing his scratched nose with a front paw.

"God is like a mother hen who calls her chicks to her and protects them," Granny explained.

Temba squatted in the dust close to the hen while the dog retreated up the road. "So that's what God is like," he said.

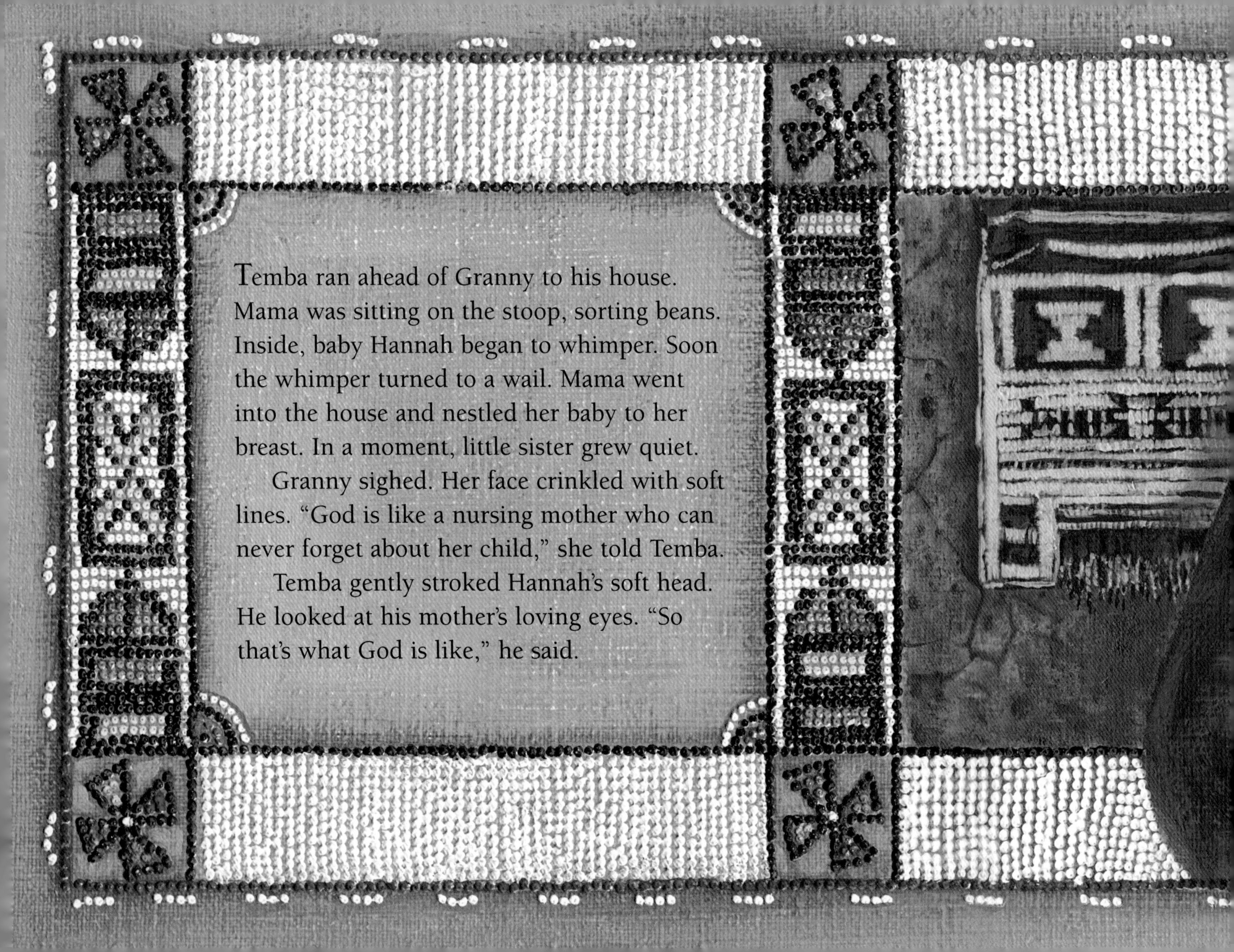

Temba ran ahead of Granny to his house. Mama was sitting on the stoop, sorting beans. Inside, baby Hannah began to whimper. Soon the whimper turned to a wail. Mama went into the house and nestled her baby to her breast. In a moment, little sister grew quiet.

Granny sighed. Her face crinkled with soft lines. "God is like a nursing mother who can never forget about her child," she told Temba.

Temba gently stroked Hannah's soft head. He looked at his mother's loving eyes. "So that's what God is like," he said.

"Can a mother forget the baby at her breast and
have no compassion on the child she has borne?
Though she may forget, I will not forget you!"
—Isaiah 49:15

"He . . . will watch over his flock like a shepherd."
—Jeremiah 31:10

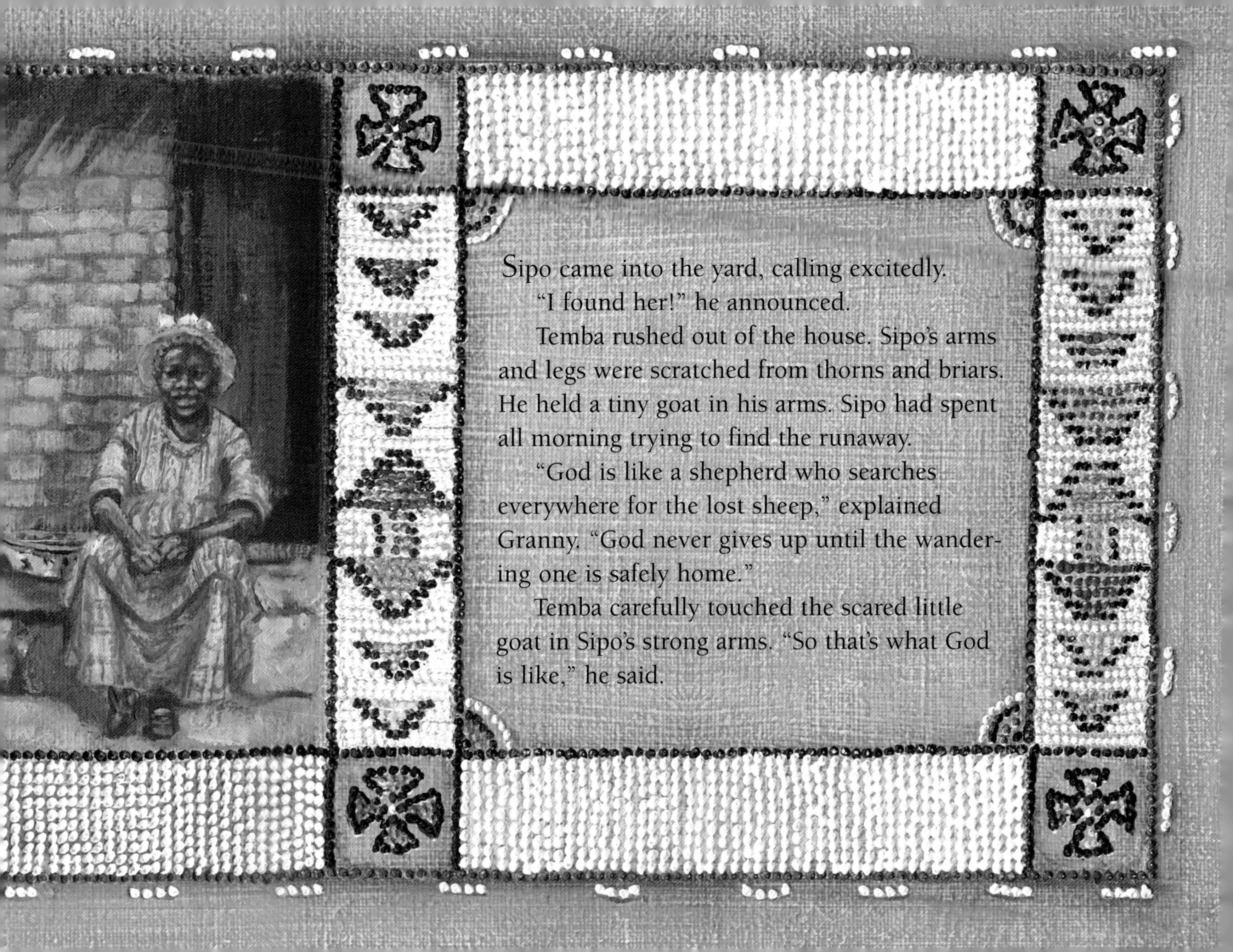

Sipo came into the yard, calling excitedly.

"I found her!" he announced.

Temba rushed out of the house. Sipo's arms and legs were scratched from thorns and briars. He held a tiny goat in his arms. Sipo had spent all morning trying to find the runaway.

"God is like a shepherd who searches everywhere for the lost sheep," explained Granny. "God never gives up until the wandering one is safely home."

Temba carefully touched the scared little goat in Sipo's strong arms. "So that's what God is like," he said.

"Granny," Temba said, sitting very close to her on the stoop. "God is like the minister, the wind, a rock, a hen, a mother, and a shepherd. God is like so many things. God must be very big."

"God is very big indeed," agreed Granny. "But God loves little chicks, little babies, little goats." She squeezed Temba tightly. "And little children."

"So that's what God is like," said Temba, and he smiled.